D1293848

The Hairy Adventures of
Harry and Stanky:
The Raunchy Rope

Dedicated to all my friends, whom I've worked with underground, and to their families who spend countless days and nights praying they'll come home alive.

Special thanks to Brooke Urbaniak for editing this book.

Printed in the United States of America

First Printing, 2020

harryandstanky@gmail.com

Harry the Bear and Stanky the dog took Jeremy
out to find a pet frog.

They hiked down the trail and out by the lake,
when Stanky ran off chasing a snake.

Stanky the dog started barking real loud, so they both ran over to see what he found.

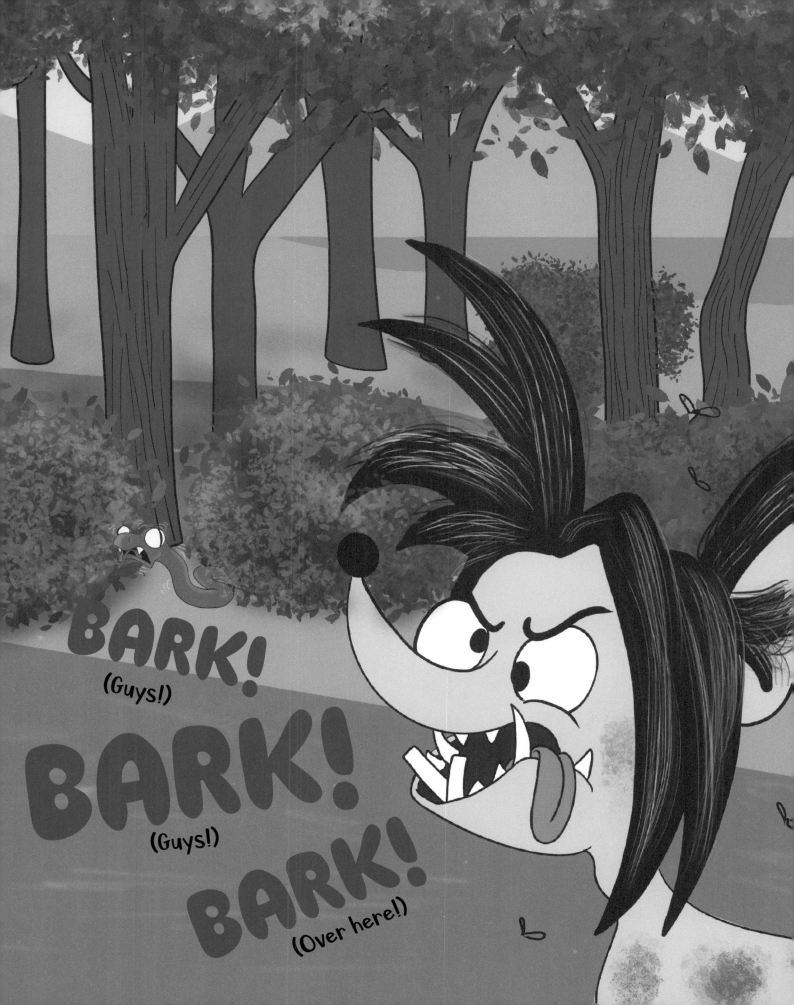

"Jeremy, my friend, did you hear that sound? I think it's deep from under the ground!"

They looked all over and what did they find? A giant hole that once was a mine.

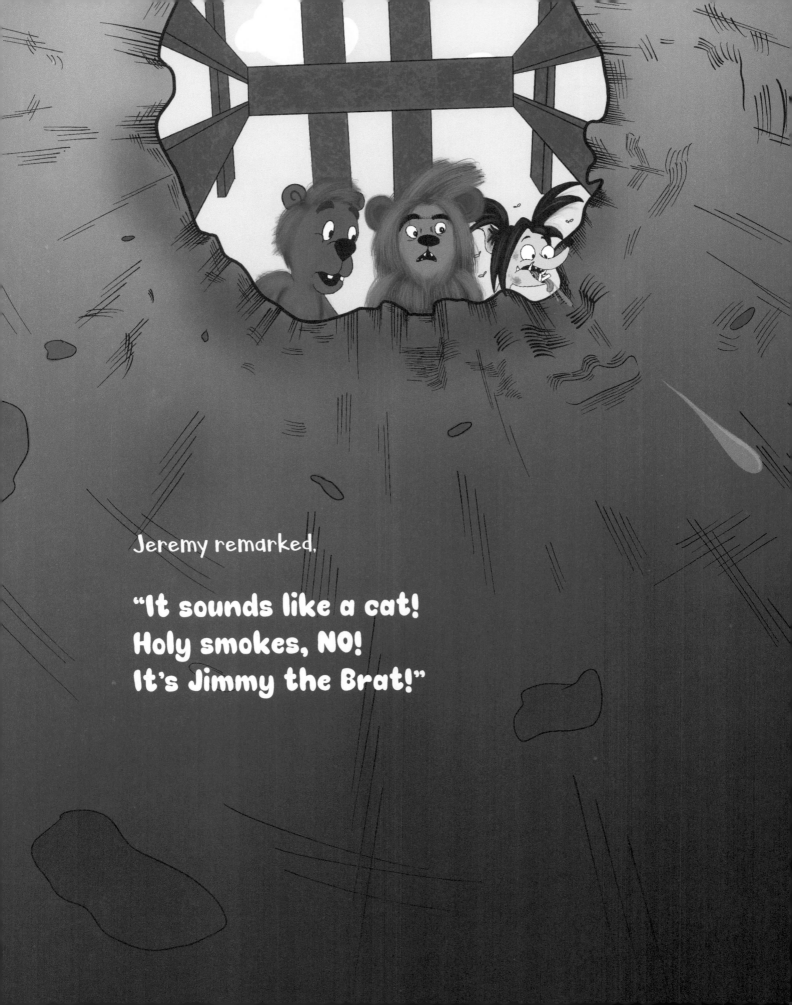

Jeremy remarked,

"It sounds like a cat!
Holy smokes, NO!
It's Jimmy the Brat!"

Jimmy the brat was a bully from school.
He picked on kids daily and thought it was cool.

He always made fun of Harry's long hair.

He threw gum in it once without any care.

"I have an idea, let's make a long rope!
The hair from my back will work, I should
hope!"

Jeremy got ready with his big sharpened claw...

He tugged and yanked
and started to saw.

They braided and weaved and tied it in knots.
It was frayed and ugly and ratty in spots.

"Jeremy! Jeremy! Look what you've done! You've shaved off all the hair on my bum!"

Jeremy laughed while pulling the rope.

"Last night in the bath, did you use any soap?!"

Jimmy had cried all the way up the
shaft. He screamed like a baby while
the other two laughed.

"Please get me out!
It's cold in here burr!
I hate the dark
and I peed on my fur!"

They laughed and hugged and gave a high five.

"Jimmy, my friend, we're so glad you're alive!"

CPSIA information can be obtained
at www.ICGtesting.com
Printed in the USA
LVHW070759061221
704865LV00037B/595